Sunny the Bunny

GOES TO CAMP

Jace Higgins & Paige Bekish

GREENLEAF
BOOK GROUP PRESS

Published by Greenleaf Book Group Press
Austin, TX
www.gbgpress.com

Distributed by Greenleaf Book Group

For ordering information or special discounts for bulk purchases, please contact Greenleaf Book Group at PO Box 91869, Austin, TX 78709, 512.891.6100.

Design and composition by Greenleaf Book Group
Cover design by Greenleaf Book Group
Illustrations by Jace Higgins and Paige Bekish

Publisher's Cataloging-in-Publication data is available.

Print ISBN: 978-1-62634-738-0
eBook ISBN: 978-1-62634-739-7

Part of the Tree Neutral® program, which offsets the number of trees consumed in the production and printing of this book by taking proactive steps, such as planting trees in direct proportion to the number of trees used: www.treeneutral.com

TreeNeutral

Manufactured through Asia Pacific Offset on acid-free paper
Manufactured in China on April 1, 2020
Batch number Q20020057

20 21 22 23 24 25   10 9 8 7 6 5 4 3 2 1

First Edition

MY NAME IS SUNNY,
and I like to bake.
I am best at making
red velvet cupcakes.

I read lots of books.
Bikes are fun too.
Sometimes I'm frightened
by things that are new.

My mom signed me up
for a camp this summer.
I am thinking that it
just might be a bummer.

She said I'll have fun,
but I am uneasy.
Even thinking of camp
makes me feel queasy.

My mom hugs me tight
and sends me away.
I am leaving for camp.
It is the first day!

I walk out the door,
then I say goodbye.
I look at my mom
and let out a sigh.

I get on the bus
and sit in the back.
It is a long ride,
so I eat a snack.

Inside my lunch box,
there are little treats.
Packed in two baggies
are carrots and beets.

When we get to camp,
there is a big crowd.
They cheer and they holler.
It is very loud.

I'm missing home,
which makes me feel sad.
I want to be with
my mom and my dad.

Now it is nighttime.
We build a fire.
Stacking the wood
higher and higher.

I am making new friends.
It is only day one.
I am starting to think
that I might have some fun.

I get a surprise.
Now I feel better!
My mom and my dad
have sent me a letter.

"Sunny, we love you.
We miss you so much.
At home, we're all good,
but please keep in touch."

My new friends and I
are ready for sports.
We grab a red ball
and head to the courts.

When we all arrive,
I stand in a square.
Then I pass the ball.
It flies through the air.

During ballet class,
I learn some new moves.
I work really hard—
my spinning improves!

At the end of class,
we all put on shows.
I watch my friend Panda
on her tippy-toes.

We head back to camp,
where our counselors say,
"We planned something fun.
Let us lead the way!"

We freeze in our tracks.
I lean forward to see
what all the good smells
could possibly be.

I see some popcorn
being passed out.
A movie is showing
about a cub scout.

I go to the lake
and wear a life vest.
I'm sailing so well.
My friends are impressed.

We eat our lunches
and nap for a while.
When I wake up,
I yawn and then smile.

I like camp so much—
I love every day.
This place is so fun,
and I want to stay!

I hop to my room
and grab all my stuff.
I need my hairbrush
to puff up my fluff.

The big camp party
is themed Hawaiian.
I get to dance with
Penguin and Lion.

At a big mountain's edge,
we rappel and climb.
After we finish,
it is almost bedtime.

We pack up our stuff
and go to our beds.
Dreams of tomorrow
fill each of our heads.

Now we are zip-lining
over the trees.
My fluff is all messy
because of the breeze.

I am really nervous
to go up so high.
My friends say, "It's fun!"
so I guess I will try.

Tonight, the event
is our camp talent show.
All my friends are here now
and ready to go.

My song won first place,
and everyone cheered.
I have already picked out
a tune for next year.

We roll out our mats,
then take puppy pose.
We stretch out our legs
and wiggle our toes.

Time to pack up.
We are going away.
Camp is now over.
It is our last day.

I grab my camp trunk
and head to the gate
where all of the grown-ups
eagerly wait.

I see my parents
and hug them so tight.
I tell them the stories
of each day and night.

I get in the car
and put on my belt.
I tell them about
the fears that I felt.

I talk about all
the good times that I had.
I am going next year,
and I am so glad.

"I did make some friends,
and memories too.
I'm no longer scared
by things that are new."

Mom says, "That's great!
I am glad you had fun.
We are so proud of you
and love you a ton!"

Acknowledgments

We are so thankful for our families' unwavering enthusiasm about the book—their love and support have been driving factors in all our success.

We also want to acknowledge our amazing publishing team, who has worked tirelessly on this project, as well as Jason Turkish, Nat Holt, Tom Klint, and the entire FCC group for their early support and belief in us.

Lastly, we would like to thank God for providing us with the necessary resources, opportunities, and friendship.

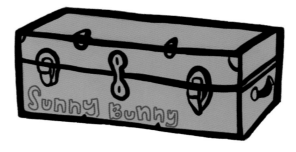

About the Authors

Jace Higgins is a sixteen-year-old high school student and an American fashion model. A four-sport varsity athlete, she enjoys running 5Ks on the weekends and is on track to complete marathons on all seven continents before the age of eighteen—earning membership into the Seven Continents Club. Jace has two bunnies and a dog. She spends her free time reading, running, doing yoga, and biking. She lives in Fort Worth, Texas, with her family, including an older and younger brother. *Photo credit: Nick Glover*

Paige Bekish is a seventeen-year-old high school student, four-sport varsity athlete, and team captain. She enjoys working with kids—regularly volunteering at her local church's nursery program and helping to organize a children's basketball program. Paige lives in Fort Worth, Texas, and loves drawing and painting. She values time with her friends and family, which includes two younger brothers. *Photo credit: Will Bekish*

Sunny the Bunny is a white Holland Lop rabbit. She was born in California, but now lives in Fort Worth, Texas, with her owner, Jace Higgins. Together, they enjoy watching movies and, of course, reading books. Sunny's favorite snacks are carrots and beets. *Photo credit: Jace Higgins*